WE LIVE HERE

FRIENDSHIP

POETRY

Stories

I GOT NEXT

BY DARIA PEOPLES-RILEY

 Greenwillow Books, *An Imprint of* HarperCollins *Publishers*

For Jaden.
He who is in you is far stronger
than anything in the world

I Got Next. Copyright © 2019 by Daria Peoples-Riley. All rights reserved. Manufactured in China. For information address
HarperCollins Children's Books, a division of HarperCollins Publishers, 195 Broadway, New York, NY 10007. www.harpercollinschildrens.com
The art was painted with black sumi ink, gouache, charcoal, and watercolor on paper, and then digitally composited in Adobe Photoshop.
The text types are Clarendon Light and Geometric 415 BT Medium.

Library of Congress Cataloging-in-Publication Data:
Names: Peoples-Riley, Daria, author, illustrator.

Title: I got next / written and illustrated by Daria Peoples-Riley.
Description: First edition. | New York, NY : Greenwillow Books, an imprint of HarperCollins Publishers, [2019] | Summary: "A young
    basketball player receives inspiration from a surprising place and joins the competition ready to try his best"— Provided by publisher.
Identifiers: LCCN 2018038690 | ISBN 9780062657770 (hardcover)
Subjects: | CYAC: Basketball—Fiction. | Self-confidence—Fiction. | Shadows—Fiction.
Classification: LCC PZ7.1.P44738 Iag 2019 | DDC [E]—dc23 LC record available at https://lccn.loc.gov/2018038690

19 20 21 22 23 SCP 10 9 8 7 6 5 4 3 2 1 First Edition

Greenwillow Books

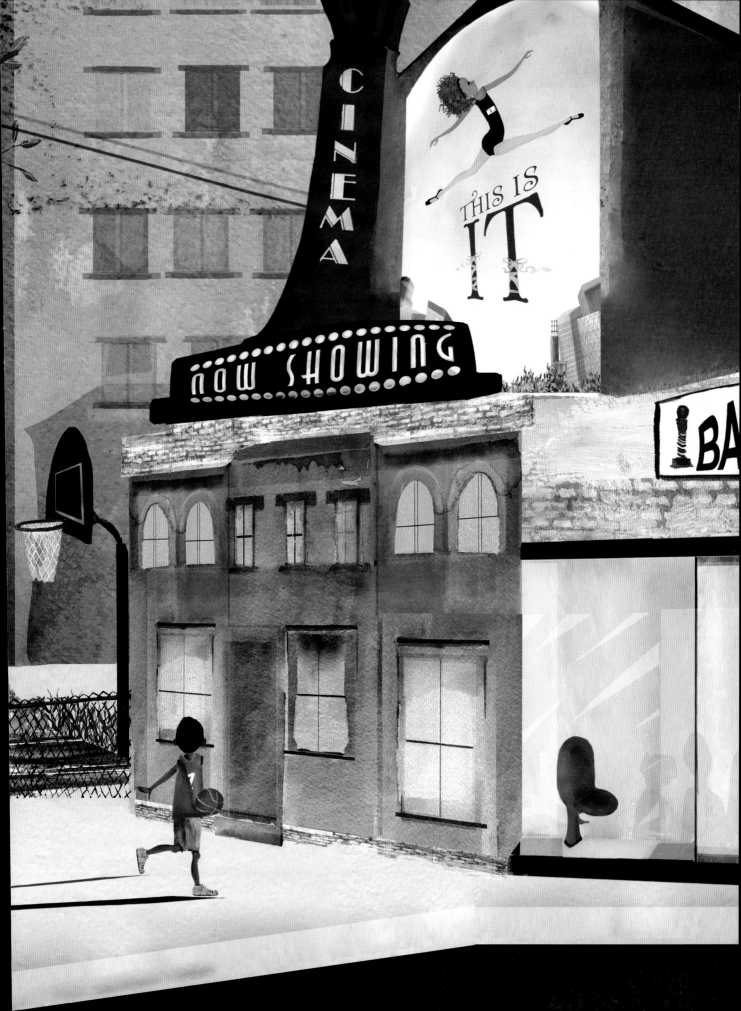

It's game day!

Time to put your
game face on!

Show me your game face!

Now you've got

your game face on!

Down by five.

Ten seconds

left to go.

Show me
what you know.

Down by two.

Now you need a stop!

Not much time
on the clock!

In. Out.
I cross 'em.
Ankles.
I break 'em.

One.
Two.

One.
Two.

I take 'em.

And one.

We won!

They might be stronger, faster, quicker—

I'll
leave
my
heart
on
the
court.

Play to win.
I am!
Fight.
All the way to the end!

Put your game face on.

Who's got next?

Let's go.

We.
GOT.
NEXT.

in loving memory of
Sonia Lynn Sadler

Forgiveness

·LOVE·

AR+

PEACE